Dear Parents:

Congratulations! Your child is taking the first steps on an exciting journey. The destination? Independent reading!

STEP INTO READING® will help your child get there. The program offers five steps to reading success. Each step includes fun stories and colorful art or photographs. In addition to original fiction and books with favorite characters, there are Step into Reading Non-Fiction Readers, Phonics Readers and Boxed Sets, Sticker Readers, and Comic Readers—a complete literacy program with something to interest every child.

Learning to Read, Step by Step!

Ready to Read   Preschool–Kindergarten
• big type and easy words • rhyme and rhythm • picture clues
For children who know the alphabet and are eager to begin reading.

Reading with Help   Preschool–Grade 1
• basic vocabulary • short sentences • simple stories
For children who recognize familiar words and sound out new words with help.

Reading on Your Own   Grades 1–3
• engaging characters • easy-to-follow plots • popular topics
For children who are ready to read on their own.

Reading Paragraphs   Grades 2–3
• challenging vocabulary • short paragraphs • exciting stories
For newly independent readers who read simple sentences with confidence.

Ready for Chapters   Grades 2–4
• chapters • longer paragraphs • full-color art
For children who want to take the plunge into chapter books but still like colorful pictures.

STEP INTO READING® is designed to give every child a successful reading experience. The grade levels are only guides; children will progress through the steps at their own speed, developing confidence in their reading. The F&P Text Level on the back cover serves as another tool to help you choose the right book for your child.

Remember, a lifetime love of reading starts with a single step!

For Christabel, Bob,
Violet, Meow-Meow,
and Bingo, who all
like snacks

Copyright © 1996 by Molly Coxe. All rights reserved. Published in the United States by Random House Children's Books, a division of Penguin Random House LLC, New York.
Step into Reading, Random House, and the Random House colophon are registered trademarks of Penguin Random House LLC.

Visit us on the Web!
StepIntoReading.com
randomhousekids.com
Educators and librarians, for a variety of teaching tools, visit us at RHTeachersLibrarians.com

Library of Congress Cataloging-in-Publication Data
Coxe, Molly. Cat traps / by Molly Coxe.
  p.   cm. — (Step into reading. A step 1 book)
Summary: A hungry cat, wanting a snack, tries to catch different animals without much success.
ISBN 978-0-679-86441-7 (trade) — ISBN 978-0-679-96441-4 (lib. bdg.) —
ISBN 978-0-307-55498-7 (ebook)
[1. Cats—Fiction. 2. Animals—Fiction. 3. Stories in rhyme.]
I. Title.   II. Series: Step into reading. Step 1 book.
PZ8.3.C8395 Cat 2003 [E]—dc21 2002152414

Printed in the United States of America   38 37 36 35 34 33 32 31 30 29

This book has been officially leveled by using the F&P Text Level Gradient™ Leveling System.

CAT TRAPS

by Molly Coxe

Random House New York

Cat wants a snack.

Cat sets a trap.

Cat gets a bug.

Ugh!

Cat wants a snack.

Cat sets a trap.

Cat gets a pig.

Too big!

Cat wants a snack.

Cat sets a trap.

Cat gets a fish.

Swish!

Cat wants a snack.

Cat sets a trap.

Cat gets a frog?

No, a dog!

Cat wants a snack.

Cat sets a trap.

Cat gets a duck.

Bad luck!

Cat wants a snack.

Cat sets a trap.

Cat gets—

a cat!

Drat.

Cat wants a snack.

Cat sets a trap.

Cat gets some chow.

Meow!